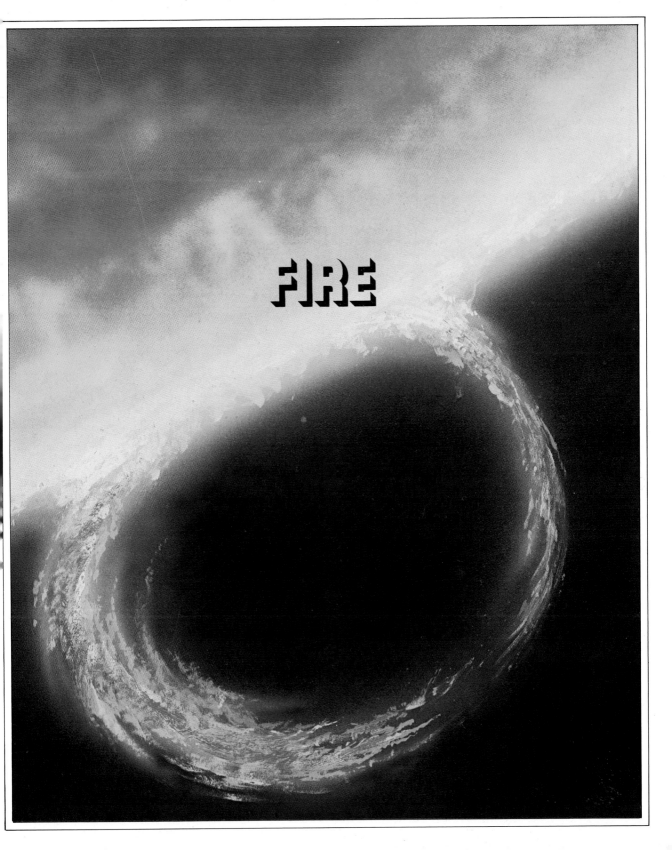

FIRE

To M.M.   J.S.

To Jamie   T.S.

First published in Great Britain by
Methuen Children's Books Ltd.
in association with Walker Books.

Text copyright © 1982 by John Satchwell
Pictures copyright © 1982 by Tom Stimpson
All rights reserved.
Library of Congress Catalog Card Number: 82-9434
Printed in Italy.
First Pied Piper printing 1984
A Pied Piper Book is a registered trademark of
The Dial Press, a division of Dell Publishing Co., Inc.,
® TM 1,163,686 and ® TM 1,054,312.

FIRE is published in a hardcover edition by
The Dial Press, 1 Dag Hammarskjold Plaza,
New York, New York 10017.
ISBN 0-8037-2552-3

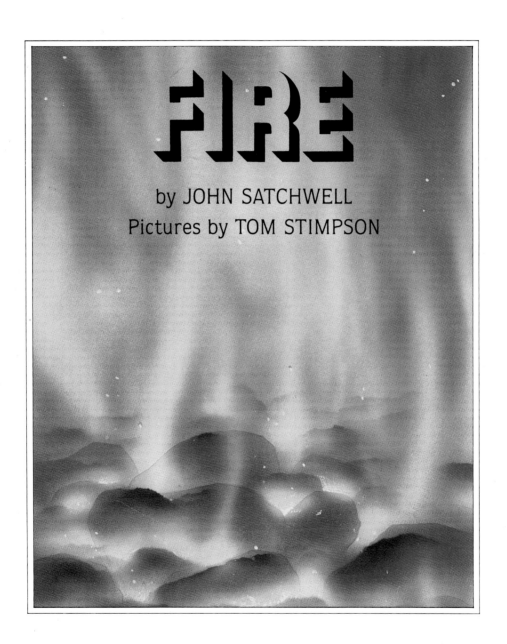

FIRE

by JOHN SATCHWELL

Pictures by TOM STIMPSON

THE DIAL PRESS/New York

Yellow flames dance upward. Their light
flickers across the faces of your friends.
You can feel the heat of the tiny flames.
Take a deep breath and blow. They waver
for an instant and then vanish. Wisps of
smoke hang in the air. Fire from a candle
looks harmless, but it is not always so
gentle. It can be as hot as a furnace or as
fierce as a rocket, as smoky as fog or
as bright as lightning.

Most things will burn if they are hot enough, even metal. The secret of making fire is in the letters *FAH*. *F* is for fuel, *A* is for air, and *H* is for heat. All must be present to start a fire. If you rub your hands together, they will get hot, but not hot enough to catch fire. Five hundred thousand years ago, people learned to make fire by rubbing dry sticks together. The sticks got hot and gave off sparks. Thin shavings of wood placed under the sticks caught the sparks and began to burn. The fire was used to give warmth and light, cook food, and frighten away wild animals.

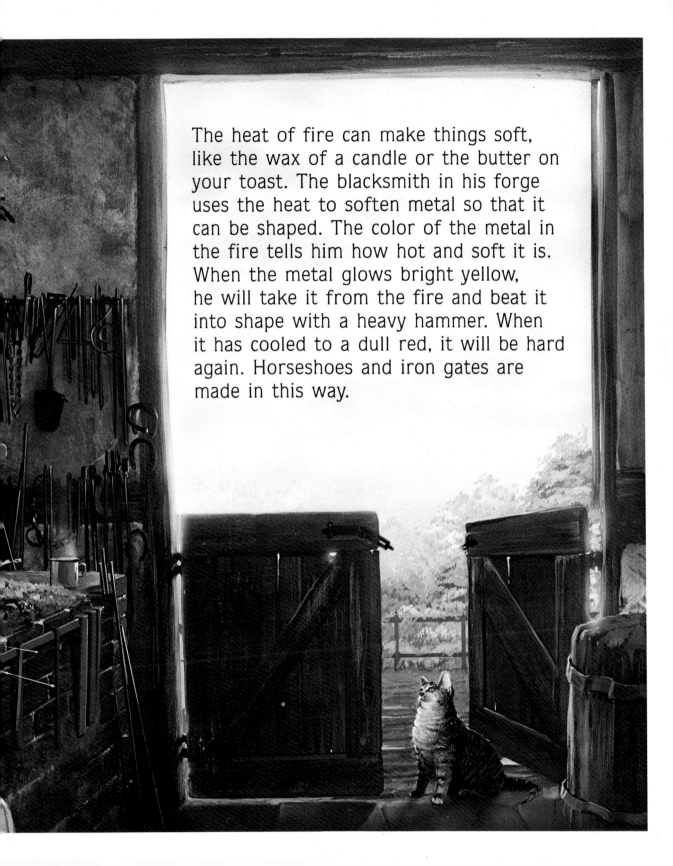

The heat of fire can make things soft, like the wax of a candle or the butter on your toast. The blacksmith in his forge uses the heat to soften metal so that it can be shaped. The color of the metal in the fire tells him how hot and soft it is. When the metal glows bright yellow, he will take it from the fire and beat it into shape with a heavy hammer. When it has cooled to a dull red, it will be hard again. Horseshoes and iron gates are made in this way.

Fire can also make machines move. Rockets use the force of burning gas to move them through space. Because there is no air in space, rockets carry their own supply in cylinders, to keep the fire burning. In a steam engine the fireman throws coal on the fire with a shovel. The burning fuel heats water in a boiler, turning it to steam. The force of the steam, released through a small pressure valve, drives the wheels. Smoke from the fire goes up the chimney, streaking out behind as the engine gathers speed.

Streams of black smoke signal that a fire is not getting enough air. The color comes from tiny pieces of unburned fuel escaping. Breathing smoke is not good for your lungs. In towns a hundred years ago people died from the choking smoke of factories that burned coal. Now there are laws that prevent unhealthful fires like this, but the air in modern towns is still dirty from the smoke given out by cars and trucks. Cigarettes have a message on their packs warning people of the dangers of inhaling their smoke.

Sometimes a fire begins by accident. Once out of control it can be very dangerous. The secret of fighting a fire is to take away one of the FAH parts that keep it going. Taking away the fuel stops it from spreading. In forest fires this means chopping down trees in its path. Smothering the fire with a blanket or soil takes away the air. Cooling it with water takes away the heat. If you are ever burned by a fire, rinse the burn with cold water for ten minutes.

Not all fires are made by people. The first fires were natural ones, created by volcanoes. Volcanoes are the chimneys of the earth, outlets from its white hot central core. In volcanic eruptions, molten rock is thrown out, setting fire to everything in its path as it streams down the mountainside. Volcanoes can also erupt under the sea, causing huge tidal waves. When the violent heat of the earth boils the water just below its surface, steam bursts out in fountains called geysers.

Lightning is another natural way that fires start. When the electricity in a thunderstorm strikes an object, it heats up and may begin to burn. If lightning strikes a dead tree, the dry wood can burst into flame. Lightning hits the highest point it can find. Many tall buildings have a lightning conductor to attract the electricity and stop it from striking the building. This is a long metal rod fixed high on the roof, which runs down to the ground. Lightning striking the conductor passes through the rod into the earth, and the building is saved.

The Ancient Greeks believed that the secret of fire was stolen from the gods. Fires were always lit at their religious festivals. At their religious center, Olympia, young men raced for the prize of a flaming torch, and the winner lit a fire to the god of the earth. Since that time, the Olympic Games have always started with the ceremony of lighting a fire. The torch itself has become a symbol of hope and peaceful achievement.

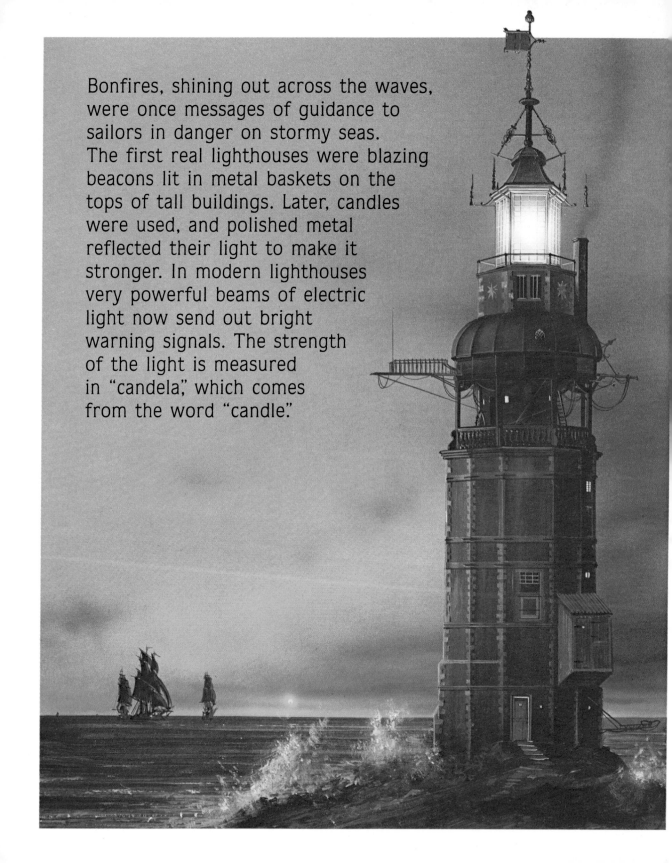

Bonfires, shining out across the waves, were once messages of guidance to sailors in danger on stormy seas. The first real lighthouses were blazing beacons lit in metal baskets on the tops of tall buildings. Later, candles were used, and polished metal reflected their light to make it stronger. In modern lighthouses very powerful beams of electric light now send out bright warning signals. The strength of the light is measured in "candela," which comes from the word "candle."

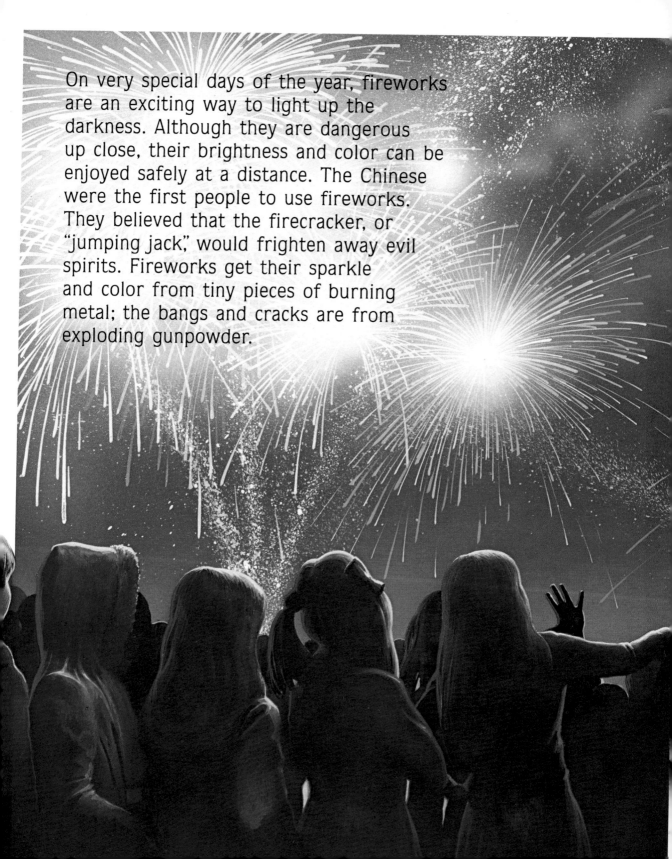

On very special days of the year, fireworks are an exciting way to light up the darkness. Although they are dangerous up close, their brightness and color can be enjoyed safely at a distance. The Chinese were the first people to use fireworks. They believed that the firecracker, or "jumping jack," would frighten away evil spirits. Fireworks get their sparkle and color from tiny pieces of burning metal; the bangs and cracks are from exploding gunpowder.

The brightest fireworks on earth are nothing compared to the sun. The sun is the hottest, brightest fire you could ever imagine. Solar flames leap thousands of miles from its surface, as it burns hydrogen gas by a method called "nuclear fusion." Unlike an ordinary fire, fusion needs no air.

The sun's warmth and light reach out to give you summer days. The sun gives life to all plants, animals, and people, and it will keep on giving life for millions of years to come.

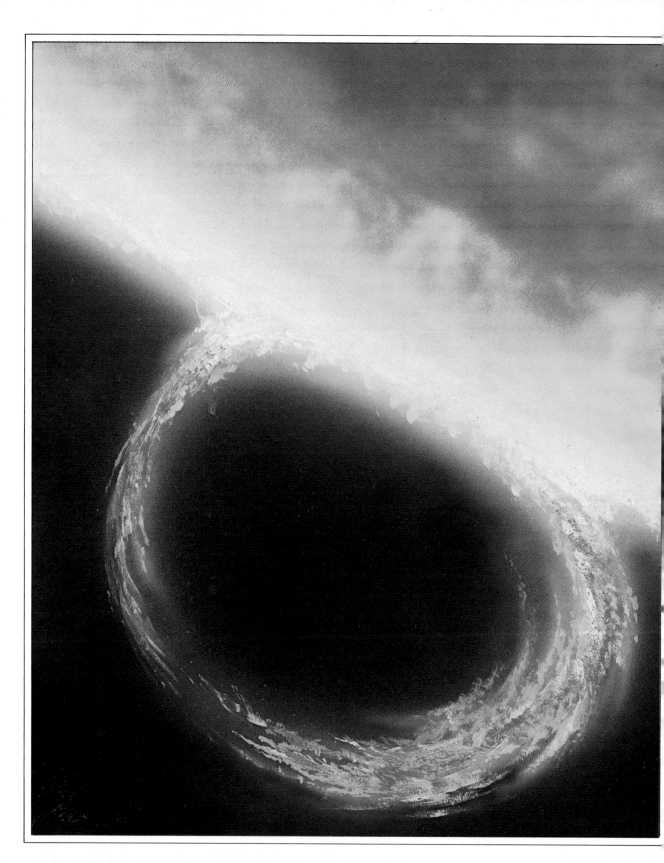